I Want A New Pet

By Sheri Henry

I asked Mom and Dad for a new pet.

They told me, "Maybe, but not yet."

Maybe because I asked for a crocodile.

They said, "It just might eat your friend Lyle."

I said I would like a horse named Ed.

They told me, "He could not sleep in your bed."

Then I wanted an eagle named Sue.

They said, "The eagle is bigger than you."

I suggested maybe I should get a tiger.

I could put a saddle on her and ride her!

I would like to have a hippopotamus named Jane.

I wonder how hard they are to tame?

An ostrich is an interesting bird.

You can actually ride them, that's what I've heard!

An elephant could be a great advantage,

although feeding him might be hard to manage.

I would like to have a dolphin named Blue.

He could be friends with me and you.

If I had a giraffe so tall,

I could ride him and see right over the wall.

A bison is like a big fluffy cow.

To take care of him, I don't know how.

If I had
a donkey
I would
name
him Jim.

I would
take very
good
care of
him.

A wolf is like a very big dog.

Instead of a stick, he could carry a log!

I think I would like to have a goose.

Or better yet, maybe a moose.

A groundhog and a woodchuck are the same thing.

If he sees his shadow, more winter he'll bring.

My mom said a shark could not live here.

On that topic, she was very clear!

A porcupine is a prickly sort,

but hugging would be a last resort!

I thought a pretty little skunk might be fun,

until he sprays you and then you are done.

I would like a raccoon named Ricky.

I have heard they can be a little tricky.

I told my parents a snake might be nice.

They told me I would have to feed him live mice!

Maybe a mouse would be a better pet?

A tiny little mouse wouldn't be a threat!

Did you know some camels have one hump and some have two?

People ride them through the desert, it's true.

A whale could be the biggest pet ever,

but we would have to live near the ocean forever.

Do you think we could find a Yeti?

We could give him his own room and feed him spaghetti!

I think I would like a cougar named Ryan.

A cougar is also called a mountain lion.

Maybe I could get a beautiful deer.

I could saddle and ride him from there to here.

I would love to learn to ride a leopard.

Or maybe I could try to be a shepherd.

Pandas look so cuddley and sweet.

Hugging one would be a treat.

A tarantula might be very cool.

I could put him in my backpack and take him to school!

A cute little fox might be a lot of fun.

We could run around and play in the sun!

Could I keep a sea lion in the pool?

Could I take him with me to school?

A chimpanzee is a curious creature.

Think of all the things I could teach her!

A Komodo dragon would be so cool.

My mom said no poisonous animals is the rule!

I would like to have a blue footed booby because I like the name.

But keeping him captive would be such a shame.

Llamas have a certain charm,

but we would need to live on a farm.

Maybe I could hang out with a gorilla?

We could sit and have tea at the villa.

What about a platypus named Gus?

A strange looking creature. Let's discuss!

If I had an orangutan, I would call him Sunshine.

We could play together all of the time.

Did you know sea turtles become adults around 30 years old?

They have a very long childhood, it's true, I am told.

A big ol' bear might be nice,

but maybe a teddy bear would suffice.

A hawk would be a cool pet.

He could see me from far away, I bet!

Baby cats are called kittens.

I could cuddle and feed her and call her Mittens.

A dog just might be the best pet ever.

Treat him well and he loves you forever!

Which pet should I get,
nobody knows.
Maybe one of each,
I suppose!

Made in the USA
Columbia, SC
04 July 2024

37959967R00027